Spaced Out

LISA THOMPSON

Illustrated by Bettina Guthridge

sundance
A Haights Cross Communications Company

The Story Characters

Jed

Comet

Jed's sister, Ali

The Story Setting

Jed's room

3

TABLE OF CONTENTS

CHAPTER 1

Jed in Space

Jed likes everything about outer space.
His room is filled with pictures of
space and spaceships.

There are glow-in-the-dark stars on the walls. Planets hang from the ceiling.

When Jed turns off his light at night,
he feels like he is floating in space.

Jed spends a lot of time looking at outer space through his telescope.

When the night sky is clear, Jed can see the surface of the moon. He can see different kinds of stars.

Ali is Jed's sister. She thinks Jed is weird for looking at outer space all of the time.

"I don't know what you think is so interesting about space," Ali says.

"That's because your brain is a vacuum," says Jed. (In space talk, vacuum means empty.)

CHAPTER 2

Collecting Moon Samples

In the backyard, there is a big pile of rocks and sand. Jed thinks it looks like the surface of the moon.

With his dog Comet, Jed spends hours collecting rock and sand samples. He feels just like a real astronaut.

Jed made his skateboard into a moon
buggy. He uses it to collect his moon
samples.

When Comet and Jed find something,
they return to the spaceship. Then they
inspect what they have found.

So far they've discovered three dog bones, a piece of limestone, two marbles, and one old coin.

What Jed wants is a real piece of space rock.

2 MarBlES

Limestone

old coin

3 dog bonES

CHAPTER 3

A Spaceship?

One night, Jed sees something that he has never seen before. A big ball of light shoots across the sky. It's bright orange and has a long tail.

It lands just behind the back fence.

Jed is scared. But he knows he has to go outside and take a look.

Jed hears noises on the other side of the fence.

Aliens, he thinks.

Maybe it is a spaceship from another planet. What if the aliens have seen Jed looking through his telescope? They might take him away and throw him into a black hole.

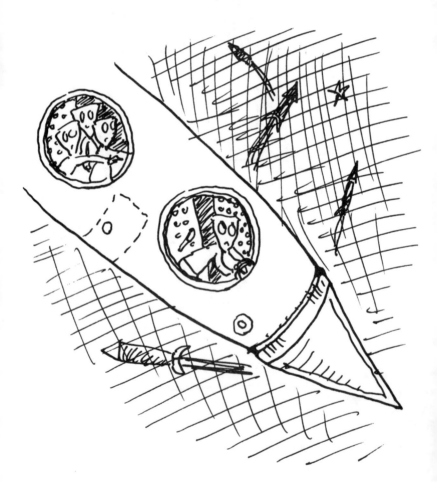

A black hole would be bad! Jed
remembered what his dad told him
about black holes. If he fell into one,
he'd end up long and thin, like a piece
of spaghetti.

But maybe they are friendly aliens,
Jed thought. Maybe they want to
take him back to their planet. He
would be famous. Then he could do
whatever he wanted.

He would spend all of his time
traveling through space and going to
new planets.

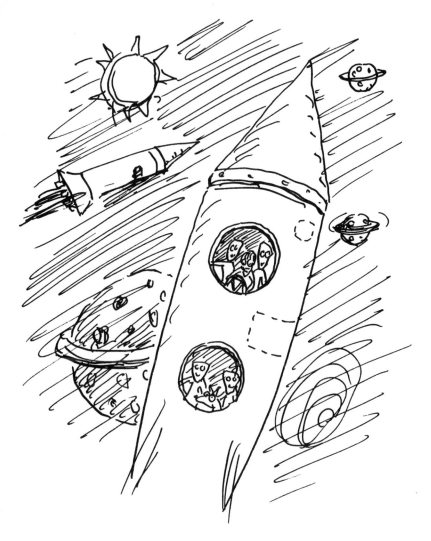

CHAPTER 4

Aliens

Jed finds a hole in the fence and bravely crawls through.

"AHHHHHHHHHHHHHHHHHHH!" he screams.

The alien has a moon-shaped head, long hair, and two big, brown eyeballs just like his own.

Jed closes his eyes and screams again.

"Stop screaming!" the alien says. It
touches his shoulder. Jed screams even
louder.

"Open your eyes!" it orders.

Jed peeks out of his right eye. Standing by his side is . . . his sister.

"What's wrong with you?" she asks. "You look all spaced out, like you just saw an alien or something."

Jed's mom and dad and sister are all staring at him. Comet is staring, too.

Jed's dad points to a hole in the ground. "Look, Jed!" he says. "A space rock landed right here."

CHAPTER 5

Space Rock

Three scientists come to look at the space rock. They do all kinds of tests on it.

Jed and Comet sit on the moon buggy
and watch.

Finally, the scientists finish.

"Everything looks safe," they say.

One of the scientists hands the rock to Jed. "Here, Jed, you can have it. It's a piece of a meteorite."

Jed can't believe it. "You mean I can keep it?" he asks.

Jed runs inside to show his mom and dad and Ali.

"Look, everyone. I get to keep the space rock. It's a meteorite."

CHAPTER 6

Be Very Careful

Later, Jed finds his sister using his telescope.

"This space stuff is so cool. There's just so much to see." Ali says, "Can I look at your meteorite?"

Jed nods. He looks at her moon-
shaped face and big, brown eyes.

He has to be careful. Maybe his sister
isn't a vacuum after all.

Maybe she is an alien!

GLOSSARY

alien
creature from
outer space

astronaut
someone who
travels into space

inspect
to look at closely

meteorite
a rock from
outer space

samples

small parts or pieces

surface

the top layer

telescope

used to look at stars

vacuum

completely empty

weird

strange

Lisa Thompson

Lisa Thompson spends a lot of her time thinking of stories and drawing pictures. She also talks very fast. Sometimes she does all three at once. When she doesn't want to think, draw, or talk, Lisa likes to run and dance. To switch off her brain and her legs, Lisa goes to sleep. Lisa is so good at sleeping that she could sleep through a hurricane.

Bettina Guthridge

Bettina used to teach Art, but loved picture books so much that she decided to start illustrating her own. She has illustrated lots of children's books. She loves wacky stories and bright colors, and she has lots of fun every day working in her studio.

Published by Sundance Publishing
One Beeman Road, P.O. Box 740, Northborough, MA 01532-0740
800-343-8204

Copyright © text Lisa Thompson
Copyright © illustrations Bettina Guthridge

First published 1999 as Sparklers by
Blake Education, Locked Bag 2022, Glebe 2037, Australia
Exclusive United States Distribution: Sundance Publishing

ISBN 0-7608-8003-4

™ sundance
A Haights Cross Communications Company